**Other CAT'S EYE Mysteries you
will enjoy:**

A CAT'S EYE Mystery

Mystery at Dark Wood

by
CAROL BEACH YORK

SCHOLASTIC INC.
New York Toronto London Auckland Sydney Tokyo

To Virginia,
affectionately

ISBN 0-590-72239-5

12 11 10 9 8 7 6 5 4 3 2 1   11   3 4 5 6 7/8

Printed in the U. S. A.   06

Commonwealth Edition

Contents

The Frightened Aunt

It was raining on the day Janie arrived at Dark Wood. The chill in the air was unusual for a summer afternoon.

Aunt Cissie met Janie's train at exactly one-twenty. She stood out of the rain in the shelter of the station platform, plump and unfashionable, twisting her handbag by its sturdy leather straps and chewing the corner of her mouth. She was going over and over in her mind whether she had been right to let Janie come for a visit. She had been over this in her mind many times in the days just past. She was not sure even now that she had done the right thing.

When the train came in sight through a blurry mist of rain in the distance, Aunt

Cissie smoothed her collar and tightened her grip on her handbag. Janie was arriving. It was too late to wonder if she had done the right thing or not.

Janie sat happily beside Aunt Cissie in the front seat of the car. Her suitcase had been put on the rear seat. The windscreen wipers swept back and forth, and through the rain-spattered glass Janie could see Dark Wood, Aunt Cissie's house, as they turned into Oak Road. The house looked large and alone in the falling rain. The nearest neighbor lived a half a kilometre away, next to Aunt Cissie's property.

Across the road was the wood, where Janie had hiked and hunted for wild flowers so many times in summers past. It was all just as she remembered it. She had been coming every summer for four years now, since she was seven, and nothing had changed.

"Nothing's changed," she said to Aunt Cissie.

Aunt Cissie was leaning forward over the wheel to see better through the rain. It took most of her concentration to drive, but after a moment she said, "Everything changes, Janie. Sometimes we just don't notice at first."

She could not stop a note of sadness from creeping into her voice. The sadness surprised Janie. It was so unlike Aunt Cissie's usually cheerful manner. Aunt Cissie was a baker-of-cakes kind of aunt. A knitter-of-mittens, a birthday-card-sender, a carer-of-baby-birds-fallen-out-of-nests, a flower-garden-planter. Absent-minded sometimes and not always getting her hat on straight. But always cheery.

This afternoon, in the gloomy rain, she sounded old and sad, and something more . . . Janie could not put her finger on what this something was exactly. But it was there, in Aunt Cissie's voice.

Aunt Cissie's house was seventy years old. Exactly the same age as Aunt Cissie (who was really Janie's great-aunt). She had lived there all her life, had grown up in it, playing in the woods and fields just as Janie loved to do when she came for her three-week visit in the summer.

Aunt Cissie had never had any brothers or sisters. An orphaned cousin had come to live with Aunt Cissie's family when Aunt Cissie was about seven years old, so it had been almost like having a sister. Cousin Emily had grown up and gone away from Dark Wood years ago, but Aunt Cissie said she herself would never leave. A widow now, Aunt Cissie had lived at Dark Wood even when she was married. She did not seem to mind that the house had grown weather-beaten and creaky and out-of-date. "We suit each other," she used to say, "this house and me. Two 'old ladies' growing older together."

Once Janie had come across a large framed photograph of Cousin Emily in the cellar at Dark Wood. Janie did not even know who it was at first, and she had asked Aunt Cissie.

"That's my Cousin Emily, who used to live here," Aunt Cissie had said. She had looked at the picture a few moments, but she had not said anything more.

Janie did not think that Cousin Emily had been very pretty. Her face was thin and solemn, her dark hair combed back severely from her forehead.

"She was about twenty when that picture was taken," Aunt Cissie had said at last. "Why, that's more than fifty years ago."

Janie had asked Aunt Cissie just where Cousin Emily lived now and if she ever came back to visit. But Aunt Cissie didn't seem to want to talk about Emily. "She went away a long time ago," Aunt Cissie said, as though that was the end of the matter.

Many years had passed since Aunt Cissie and Emily had been children. The old house stood on through the years, through snowstorms and baking summer sun, until its painted boards peeled, were painted again, and peeled once more. Until its back steps sagged and its windows shuddered and rattled in the wind. Until it was a landmark that everyone knew — Dark Wood, the old country home on Oak Road. Aunt Cissie's house.

Inside the house, everything was so old-fashioned, compared to the block of flats where Janie lived at home, that it was like stepping into a time machine. There was a parlour with an old spinet piano and a beautiful antique clock on the mantel. Also on the ground floor there was a dining room with a huge bay window, and a big kitchen with a round oak table in the middle of the floor, and pots of geraniums on the windowsills. Downstairs in the cellar there were shelves of plum jam and tomato preserves, put up by Aunt Cissie herself. It was always cool in the cellar, even on the hottest summer days — and sometimes mice were there, scampering out of sight across the hard earth floor when they heard a step on the stair.

Upstairs there were four bedrooms along

the hallway. Two were closed up and never used anymore. Of the other two, one was Aunt Cissie's and one was what she called the spare room. It was Janie's room when she visited Aunt Cissie, a small blue and white room with a sloping ceiling and a blue hooked rug on the old varnished floor.

Usually it was a bright room, with the east windows full of sunlight in the morning. But today, in the rain, it had a dark cosiness about it, and it seemed to Janie that the room closed about her welcomingly. When Aunt Cissie turned on the lamp, a warm pool of light fell on the blue quilt folded at the foot of the bed. Nothing had changed. It was all just as Janie remembered it.

Janie opened her smaller suitcase first, because she had put a present for Aunt Cissie in that one, on top of her carefully folded shorts and blouses and pyjamas. It was a glass paperweight with flowers imbedded inside in the heavy glass. Janie had picked it out herself, and her mother had said she was sure Aunt Cissie would like it. "And I think she needs a paperweight," Janie's mother had added. "Her desk always seems to have loose papers and things cluttering it up."

"It's so pretty, Janie," Aunt Cissie said, when she had taken away the tissue-paper wrapping from the paperweight.

Janie beamed under Aunt Cissie's approval, her freckled face upturned. Aunt Cissie's fingers smoothed the cool surface of the glass, and her expression was all the thanks Janie really needed.

Janie began to take her things out of the suitcases. Through the window she saw the postman's car by the postbox on the road. He was late today because of the rain, which glistened on the black car roof.

"Your post's here," she said to Aunt Cissie, who sat watching her unpack. "I'll run out and get it for you —" But Janie stopped when she saw Aunt Cissie's face. The happiness had fallen away, and her eyes were frightened. Suddenly Janie realised what had been in Aunt Cissie's voice besides the sadness: It had been *fear*. But what could Aunt Cissie be frightened of? . . . Why would anybody be afraid of the post?

"Don't you want me to get it?"

Aunt Cissie made an effort to smile. "Of course, dear, of course I do. It's just — just that it's raining —"

"I don't mind."

Janie started out of the room, and Aunt Cissie said, "Take an umbrella, dear —"

But Janie didn't bother. She liked running through the rain. And anyway, it was a family joke that Aunt Cissie never could find an umbrella when she needed it.

When Janie brought in the post (a newspaper, a postcard from a friend travelling in Mexico, and a large, white envelope), Aunt Cissie was in the kitchen. The rain had made the room dark, and Aunt Cissie had turned on the overhead lamp. She did not seem to want to see the post.

"Just put it anywhere," she said to Janie. "I'm making tea now, and that's more important."

But Janie saw that she was looking at the post as Janie put it on the kitchen table. And Aunt Cissie's hand on the teapot was trembling.

Watching

The letter was very short. Only one sentence.

I AM WATCHING YOU

The words were printed in large, rough letters across the entire page. Janie read it without really meaning to. She certainly knew better than to pry into other people's post. But when Aunt Cissie had taken the letter out of the large, white envelope and read that one big, scrawly sentence, she had let the paper slip from her fingers and fall on the table by her cup. Janie had glanced down — and then she couldn't help reading what was written because the letters were so large.

"Oh, dear." A sigh escaped Aunt Cissie's lips. She sat staring in front of her, her mind

— it seemed to Janie — far away from that kitchen with the rain-streaked windows and the kettle hissing on the stove.

"Is anything wrong?" Janie asked. She longed to reach out and pat Aunt Cissie's hand. Aunt Cissie looked so frightened and downcast.

Aunt Cissie looked at Janie with bemusement, as if she just remembered that Janie was there.

"What, dear? Wrong? Oh, no — well, I don't know, I'm not sure . . ." Her voice wavered off with confusion, and she shook her head helplessly.

Janie waited, and after a moment Aunt Cissie said, "I just don't know what to make of it." She looked down at the letter with its one sentence, but she did not pick it up again.

"It's the fourth one," she said to Janie. But this didn't explain much to Janie.

"What does it mean?" Janie asked.

Aunt Cissie only shook her head and sighed again. "I don't know, dear. But it frightens me." Her lips trembled.

Janie felt her heart stop a moment to hear Aunt Cissie say that — dear, sweet Aunt Cissie. That anyone would want to frighten her was the last thing Janie could imagine.

"The first letter was the same as this, and

unsigned, like this one. I AM WATCHING YOU. Then the second letter said, YOU KNOW WHAT I WANT, and the third letter said, I AM WAITING. And now this, the same message again."

"Who is watching you?" Janie could not help asking. But it was, of course, a foolish question. Aunt Cissie had said the letters were unsigned.

The kitchen now seemed eerie in the lamplight, with the rain falling outside and the letter between them on the table. Janie could feel her arms prickling with sudden cold.

"It's an awful feeling, Janie," Aunt Cissie said softly and sadly. "At night I can hear the wind outside, and this old house creaks and groans like old houses do, even in the middle of the night when nobody is walking about. And I listen to the wind at the windows, and the house creaking, and I'm sure someone is by the window or at my door, watching me — waiting for something —"

Janie hunched in her chair, staring at Aunt Cissie. A tear welled in the old lady's eye. "I was going to write to your mother and tell her that perhaps you had better not come for your visit, but I knew how much you looked forward to it, and I would have missed seeing you." Aunt Cissie paused, and then went on unsteadily. "I persuaded myself that the first and second letters were just mistakes or somebody playing a joke. They were several days apart. But the third letter came yesterday, and it didn't seem so easy to think it was a mistake or a joke after all. And now this one today — oh, dear, I just don't know what to do. I don't know if you should stay —"

Janie felt stunned to think she might have to go home or that she might have missed her visit to Aunt Cissie's altogether. All last week she had been packing and making plans and saying good-bye to her friends. And Aunt Cissie had actually been thinking about telling her not to come.

"Why don't we call the police?" Janie suggested hastily. She thought surely they could solve the mystery. She certainly did not want to be sent home! It would be bad enough to miss her visit — but it would be worse to go away and leave Aunt Cissie alone when she was in trouble.

"I suppose that's the best thing to do," Aunt Cissie agreed slowly. "I thought of going to the police when the second letter came, but sometimes, on sunny mornings when no letter came in the post, all my fears seemed silly. It was at night, when I'd gone to bed, that I felt uneasy in the dark, and I'd think, well, tomorrow I'll go and see Tom Hadley. He's our police chief. But then morning would come, and I'd think, no, it's all just some silly joke, and I don't want the whole police force laughing at me again. I guess they think I'm funny enough already."

"Why do they think you're funny?"

Aunt Cissie hesitated. "Well," she admitted, "I threw some tomatoes at Mr. Johnson's cats, and he reported it to the police. Tom Hadley sent a man out to see what was going on, and he said he'd never met anybody who threw tomatoes at cats. He laughed and laughed. I thought he'd fall right off the front porch, he laughed so hard." Aunt Cissie's voice had a touch of exasperation.

"Why did you throw tomatoes at the cats?"

"They come around my garden after the birds, and sometimes that's the handiest thing I can put my hands on. I wouldn't want to throw anything too hard that would really hurt the cats. I just want to scare them away."

Janie knew from her past visits that Aunt Cissie always kept three or four bird feeders in her garden, and it upset her if any cats or dogs strayed into the garden and bothered the birds.

"Mr. Johnson lives in that next house down the road, you know," Aunt Cissie explained, "and we never have got on together. He's angry because I don't cut down the trees along my property line. Says they shade his garden and nothing will grow properly there. Oh, we've had our differences over the years. Anyway, I'd hate to have that same policeman laughing at me again."

But contacting the police did seem the best thing to do. There was a Quilt and Bake Sale in town the next afternoon, an annual affair that Aunt Cissie and Janie never missed. Aunt Cissie said she would stop at the police station on the way.

Janie settled into bed that night thinking about so many things that she thought she would never get to sleep. She thought about all the things she wanted to do this summer at Aunt Cissie's (if she didn't have to go home!), and she thought about the four mysterious letters.

And then she thought that if someone was watching Aunt Cissie, then someone was watching her, too. It was a nasty feeling. Janie pulled the covers up over her head and took a long time to get to sleep that night.

A Visit to the Police

Just as Aunt Cissie had said, when morning came the fears of the night before faded a little. It was a bright, sunny day — all the rain over. As Janie ate her breakfast at Aunt Cissie's big kitchen table, it was hard to think that anybody could wish Aunt Cissie harm. Nor did it seem likely that any unfriendly figures lurked behind the trees that dotted the sunny garden round the house.

Birds twittered in the tree branches, and the only person Janie and Aunt Cissie saw all morning was the postman. Janie ran down to the road for the post, and there was no mysterious letter for Aunt Cissie. There was only a telephone bill and an advertisement for flower seeds.

About noon they set out for town in Aunt Cissie's car. Aunt Cissie had the four mysterious letters in her purse, held together by a wide rubber band. Her heart beat faster every time she thought about them. Her hat was on a little crooked, and she had forgotten her gloves. But then it wasn't every day she went to the police.

Janie watched the road stretching ahead in the sunlight. She had never been to a police station before, and she felt a shiver of excitement go down her back as she thought about it.

Chief Hadley himself said he would handle the matter, when Aunt Cissie announced that she had come about some letters she had received. It didn't appear to be a very busy day around the station. Several policemen were lounging in the outer room. As Aunt Cissie went by, following Chief Hadley back to his office, one of the men said, "Thrown any more tomatoes, Mrs. Mariott?"

He was a short, stocky young man with reddish hair and mischievous blue eyes.

Aunt Cissie fluttered one ungloved hand in his direction and sailed by. Janie frowned. The policeman didn't seem to know a frown when he saw one, and he winked at Janie in a friendly way. She stayed close behind Aunt Cissie, because Aunt Cissie had said Janie could come along to Chief Hadley's office if she wanted to. And of course she wanted to. She had never been back into the private office of a chief of police before!

"Now let's see what we have here," Chief Hadley said, settling himself into the chair behind his desk. He was a big, grey-haired man with dark, bushy eyebrows.

There were several other chairs by the desk, and Janie and Aunt Cissie sat down, too. Aunt Cissie carefully unfolded her letters and laid them out on the desk for Chief Hadley to see.

"This is the order they came in?"

"Yes," Aunt Cissie said. "I AM WATCHING YOU. YOU KNOW WHAT I WANT. I AM WAITING, and then yesterday another the same as the first, I AM WATCHING YOU."

Chief Hadley pursed his lips together thoughtfully and stared down at the letters on his desk. He didn't seem about to laugh at all. He didn't seem to think there was anything humorous about Aunt Cissie and her letters. The office was very silent.

After what seemed a long time, Chief Hadley said, "Do you have any idea at all, Mrs. Mariott, who might have sent these letters?"

Aunt Cissie shook her head. "No, I don't,

no idea at all. I wasn't even frightened at first. I thought it was just a mistake or a joke. But now, well, I don't know what to think. Four seem too many for a mistake, and if it's a joke I think it's a poor one."

"I think so, too," Chief Hadley said. He smiled faintly as he said that, but he was not laughing at Aunt Cissie.

In fact, there was such a serious expression in his kindly eyes that Janie began to be even more frightened than the night before. She had thought that seeing the police would somehow take care of everything. But now she was beginning to feel scared again in the middle of the sunny day.

"Anybody angry at you about anything?" Chief Hadley asked. "Maybe somebody you've had a disagreement with about something, like Mr. Johnson and his cats."

"Well, yes, there's that." Aunt Cissie nodded reluctantly. "But we've had trouble off and on for the last forty years or so, and he's never written me letters about it."

"You never know," Chief Hadley said. "Anyway, that was just an example. Can you think of anyone else who might be angry at you about anything and want to make you frightened or unhappy?"

Aunt Cissie started to say no, and then she stopped. "There was that Mrs. Arnot," she said thoughtfully. "You know, Mrs. Arnot who has the antique shop on Lincoln Street."

"What about Mrs. Arnot?" Chief Hadley listened to Aunt Cissy closely.

"She came around a few weeks ago and wanted to buy my house," Aunt Cissie explained. "She said her shop wasn't nearly big enough for her business, it's growing so, and she thought Dark Wood might be a good setting for antiques. She said she would make it into a salesroom downstairs, and live upstairs — or something like that. Anyway, I hardly listened to her. I told her I wasn't remotely interested in selling my house. I told her I'd lived in it since the day I was born and I intend to live in it until the day I die."

"How did she act when you said you didn't want to sell?" Chief Hadley asked.

"She didn't like it very much," Aunt Cissie admitted. "She said something about not giving up and how I might change my mind. Naturally, I told her not to have any false hopes that I would change my mind, but I'm not sure how much she was impressed by what I said. She's a rather forceful woman, Mr.

Hadley," Aunt Cissie added confidingly. "Used to having things her way, I'd say."

"She's a hard businesswoman, I hear." Chief Hadley nodded understandingly.

"Very forceful," Aunt Cissie repeated. She shifted in the uncomfortable wooden chair. "I felt worn out when she finally left, and I certainly hope she never comes back to see if I've changed my mind."

Chief Hadley had picked up a pencil, and he tapped it against the edge of the desk a few moments, watching Aunt Cissie's worried old face as she talked. After she told him about Mrs. Arnot, he tried to get her to think if there was anybody else who might bear some ill feeling toward her for any reason, but Aunt Cissie could not think of anyone else.

Then Chief Hadley said suddenly, "I'll bet this little lady's eager to get on her way to the quilt fair." He stood up, smiling at Janie, who had sat quietly throughout the conversation.

"We haven't missed one in the four years since Janie's been coming to visit me," Aunt Cissie said. "And I haven't missed one myself since they started. Must be twelve or thirteen years now. All I know is, I've got more quilts than I know what to do with."

Chief Hadley chuckled. Only for a moment

did his face grow serious again as he glanced back at the letters on the desk. "Let me keep these," he said to Aunt Cissie, "and see what I can turn up."

Aunt Cissie nodded absently. She didn't want to take the awful letters home with her anyway. She never even wanted to see them again.

"Now you two just go right ahead and have a good time," Chief Hadley said. "Don't let these letters spoil your afternoon."

Aunt Cissie straightened her hat and held out her hand to Chief Hadley. "You've been very kind," she said, and he patted her hand reassuringly.

"You come and see me anytime you're troubled about anything," he said.

But somehow Janie did not feel as comforted as she had expected to feel. Nor did Aunt Cissie. They came outside into the bright sunlight, blinking for a few moments after the dimmer light of the police station and Chief Hadley's office. Something in Chief Hadley's manner hovered over them. He was worried about the letters, and his telling them to go to the quilt sale and enjoy themselves had sounded as though he was trying to cover up the worry he felt.

"Well," said Aunt Cissie, gripping her handbag and squinting through the sunlight toward the car parked at the kerb, "I think we'd better be on our way, Janie."

Janie trailed after Aunt Cissie. When they drove off she saw Chief Hadley standing in the doorway talking to one of the policemen. They both watched Aunt Cissie's car as it drove away.

"I Will Be Back"

The Quilt and Bake Sale was held in Ransome Park, at the edge of town. Janie and Aunt Cissie met her friend Mrs. Witticomb at the quilt stalls at one o'clock, just as Aunt Cissie had arranged. Janie saw Mrs. Witticomb first and tugged at Aunt Cissie's arm. "There she is, Aunt Cissie."

Janie had met Mrs. Witticomb in past summers. She was someone it was not easy to forget. Mrs. Witticomb was a heavy woman with a mound of beautiful white hair. Her dresses were usually long and flowing, and Mrs. Witticomb herself, in warm weather, tended to be flushed and moist-looking. She surged along through the summer heat like a battleship churning through rough waters.

Beside her, as usual, was Miss Perry, her companion, chauffeur, and housekeeper. Miss Perry was younger, slimmer, and always cool-looking. Her dark hair was combed neatly (although in a rather plain fashion). She wore a single strand of pearls and small pearl earrings, like a uniform.

Mrs. Witticomb had a gigantic leaf-shaped fan in her grasp, and a limp handkerchief in the other hand, with which she dabbed at her perspiring face.

Miss Perry was wearing dark glasses, which to Janie was like looking into a blank face. She might not have recognised Miss Perry with the dark glasses, but there was no missing Mrs. Witticomb.

Mrs. Witticomb patted Janie on the head with her handkerchief and said, "Well, well, another year gone by, eh, Janie? I'm glad you're here to keep an eye on Cissie for us." And she winked broadly with one great, bright blue eye.

Miss Perry drifted away to follow her own pursuits at the stalls. Aunt Cissie told Mrs. Witticomb about her visit to Chief Hadley.

Mrs. Witticomb fanned herself and kept saying, "Yes, yes, yes," as Aunt Cissie's story unfolded.

At two o'clock they ate a picnic lunch under the trees. And during the game hour, Janie won a prize in the peanut-hop, a game played by carrying a peanut in a teaspoon across the park and back while hopping on one foot.

At last, as the afternoon drew on toward suppertime, Aunt Cissie said she thought they had better get home. They left Mrs. Witticomb and Miss Perry and drove through the quiet afternoon toward Oak Road. The countryside shimmered in the late afternoon sunlight, the road gleamed. When they turned on to Oak Road and Dark Wood came into sight, the sun was hitting the windows of the house so that each pane was like a sheet of gold. Bathed in the sunlight the old house did not look so weather-worn and faded. The trees in the yard cast sun-dappled shadows across the grass. Janie felt her breath draw in — it was such a beautiful sight.

Inside was less beautiful.

Inside was a mess.

Someone had been inside Aunt Cissie's house while they were gone.

Drawers were opened and the contents spilled on the floor.

Books had been knocked off the bookshelves.

Chair cushions had been turned over.

Lampshades were taken from the lamps.

It was a horrifying thing to see, as Janie and Aunt Cissie came in and stood in the parlour doorway.

"Why — why — what's happened —" Aunt Cissie could hardly speak.

Janie's eyes were as wide as saucers, her face pale beneath the freckles.

They went through all the downstairs rooms. Even the kitchen had been upset. It looked as though someone had been searching for something in Aunt Cissie's house.

On the top of Aunt Cissie's big round kitchen table was a note, scrawled in the same large, ragged letters as the messages that had come in the post. This message said:

I WILL BE BACK

The Intruder

Tears came slowly into Aunt Cissie's gentle, old eyes as she looked around her beloved house and saw the way her things had been tossed around. The tears overflowed her eyes and spilled down her cheeks.

About the time that Janie saw the tears on Aunt Cissie's cheeks, Janie realised that there were tears in her own eyes, too. Tears of fright and confusion that anyone could do something like this to Aunt Cissie's house. It was a very nasty feeling to come into a house and see that someone had been there pawing around while you'd been gone, while you thought your house was waiting quietly and peacefully for your return.

Aunt Cissie sat down in the rocking chair

in the parlour and took a handkerchief from her pocket and looked around. Janie sat on the footstool beside her and said, "Don't cry, Aunt Cissie."

Aunt Cissie sniffled and dabbed at her nose with her handkerchief. By and by she said, "You're right, Janie — we can't sit here crying like two ninnies, can we?"

"Call the police," Janie said. It seemed as if that was the only thing she could think of to say since she had arrived at Aunt Cissie's. ("You've been watching too many television shows," she thought her father would say if he heard her.)

Aunt Cissie made an effort to dry her tears and pull herself together. But even so, her hand trembled as she lifted the phone to make her call to the police. And her voice sounded frail and wavery when she asked to speak to Chief Hadley. Janie huddled on the footstool by the phone table and admired Aunt Cissie for making the phone call when she was still so upset.

When Aunt Cissie hung up, she said to Janie, "Tom Hadley says not to touch anything until he comes. He wants to see things just the way they were left by the" — Aunt Cissie hesitated — "by the intruder. That's what he called it

— the intruder. Oh, Janie" — Aunt Cissie reached out and hugged the girl close to her — "I feel that someone hates me — and I don't know why — but they hate me — I feel it." And she began to cry again as she looked about the ravaged room.

If Janie thought Chief Hadley had looked serious when Aunt Cissie showed him her four letters, it was nothing to how serious he looked when he stood in Aunt Cissie's parlour and saw the open desk drawers, the scattered papers and overturned ornaments, the disarray of books and chair cushions. He strode through the dining room and the kitchen.

He had brought another policeman with him, the red-haired one who had teased Aunt Cissie about throwing tomatoes at cats. His name was Sergeant Denton, and Chief Hadley sent him upstairs to look around. He came down almost at once and said that the intruder had not been upstairs. Everything there was still in order.

Chief Hadley and Sergeant Denton went downstairs into the cellar, but there did not seem to be anything disturbed there either.

Maybe that's what the note means, Janie thought to herself. Whoever it was has to come back because he didn't find what he wanted. He didn't have time to go upstairs or into the cellar.

Chief Hadley took the note to put with the other notes that Aunt Cissie had received.

"Who knew you were going to be gone today?" he asked Aunt Cissie. His forehead was creased with a deep frown of dissatisfaction.

"Why, everybody who knows me, I suppose," Aunt Cissie replied forlornly. "Everybody knows I never miss the quilt sale."

Chief Hadley shook his head glumly. "That doesn't narrow things down much."

"Did you lock your doors, Mrs. Mariott?" he asked next. "I noticed that the kitchen door is unlocked now."

"Oh, dear," Aunt Cissie exclaimed with dismay. "Is the kitchen door unlocked? Then we must have left it that way, because we went out of the front door and I know I locked that. I had to get out my key when we came home."

"You're sure the front door was locked?"

"Yes." Aunt Cissie nodded emphatically. "I couldn't find my key at first, so I tried the knob because sometimes I do go off and forget to lock up —" She paused and glanced down guiltily. People were always scolding her about forgetting to lock her doors when she went out. "But, anyway, it *was* locked, so I hunted in my handbag some more and, of course, I found the key. I suppose the back door was unlocked all the time. I just didn't realise it."

Chief Hadley shook his head. "Well, I think that answers the question of how the intruder entered." His expression seemed to say that it was too late now to scold Aunt Cissie.

Sergeant Denton helped Janie put books back on the shelves and straighten the rooms, and Chief Hadley questioned Aunt Cissie for a long time about what someone could possibly have been looking for in her house. Aunt Cissie couldn't think of anything unusual that anyone would want to steal. Nothing seemed to be missing. When he left, Chief Hadley asked Aunt Cissie to notify him if she did discover that something had been taken.

"I will," Aunt Cissie promised. But she never did find anything missing or think of anything that anyone could have wanted to take.

Sergeant Denton was assigned to stay at Dark Wood, in case the intruder did return.

If Janie thought she had had trouble going to sleep the night before, it was even harder this second night. She could hear Aunt Cissie and Sergeant Denton talking for a while, and she was still awake when Aunt Cissie went to bed. After that the house was very quiet, and Janie thought about Sergeant Denton downstairs, keeping watch.

Twice Janie got out of bed and looked out of her window across the dark garden around the house to see if she could spot anyone hiding there. The trees stood out as darker shapes in the darkness. Beyond the garden the countryside dissolved into a darkness too black to see anything. Was someone out there somewhere? Janie wondered. Watching Dark Wood, planning to return . . .

Janie's List

The next morning Mrs. Follett, whose house was behind Aunt Cissie's property, came over to see what was going on. News had travelled that Aunt Cissie's house had been robbed.

"I don't think you can say it's been robbed, if nothing's been taken," Aunt Cissie said to her.

Mrs. Follett was a small, pretty woman, a little older than Janie's mother. Janie remembered her from past summers. She came over to visit Aunt Cissie every few days. Mrs. Follett had two sons, and while she visited she was usually knitting a scarf or a sweater or a pair of gloves.

She was in the kitchen with Aunt Cissie and Janie when Chief Hadley came. "I've been thinking," he began. "I think that note, I WILL BE BACK, was just to scare you. Anyone really planning to return wouldn't make such a point of alerting you. First thing you'd do is have someone like Sergeant Denton here. Whoever it is just wants to keep you uneasy and wondering."

Mrs. Follett nodded. "That sounds logical," she agreed.

"And I don't think they were looking for anything," Chief Hadley continued. "They just wanted you to think they were."

"Then you don't think the — the intruder will return?" Aunt Cissie asked.

"No, I really don't, at least not the way you'd expect. First the letters, then the search of the house. The next thing will be something different still."

"The next thing?" Aunt Cissie clutched her hands together in distress. "Do you think there will be something *more*?"

Mrs. Follett's dark eyes widened with concern. "Oh, Mr. Hadley," she said.

"I don't mean to alarm you," he said. "There may be nothing further at all. I was just pointing out that I don't expect another search of the house. But I can leave Sergeant Denton here again tonight, if it would make you feel safer."

"Why couldn't my boys come over for a few nights?" Mrs. Follett suggested. Her sons, Dave and Jon, were eighteen and sixteen years old.

"That would be comforting," Aunt Cissie said gratefully.

"Good." Chief Hadley stood up. "I'll have the police car patrol during the night just to keep an eye on things, and you let me know if anything unusual happens, no matter how small."

"I will," Aunt Cissie promised.

Later that morning Janie decided to make a list of people who might want to frighten Aunt Cissie. She began with Mr. Johnson who lived down the road and let his cats wander into her aunt's yard. Janie remembered seeing him a few times in past summers, a tall, ruddy man with white hair. His wife was fat and wore glasses with steel rims that glittered in the light.

Janie put Mr. and Mrs. Johnson at the head of her list of suspects.

Next she put Mrs. Arnot, who wanted to buy Aunt Cissie's house for an antique shop. Mrs. Arnot could be angry because Aunt Cissie wouldn't sell her house. Maybe she was trying to frighten her away.

This made Janie think of something else, something she had not thought of before. She hurried downstairs and found Aunt Cissie alone in the parlour, sitting rather forlornly by the window in her rocking chair.

"Aunt Cissie," Janie began in a rush, "didn't you tell me last summer that the Folletts wanted to buy some land between your house and theirs, to make their farm bigger?"

"Why, yes, they did, Janie. But I told them I couldn't sell any of the land. It's like part of me after all these years. They understand."

"But do they still want to buy it?"

"I expect they would still buy it if I'd change my mind and sell it to them. But we don't discuss it anymore."

"But maybe they're really angry that you won't sell," Janie said. "They know you aren't using the land for farming or anything. Maybe they're just pretending to be nice and friendly, and they're really terribly angry about it."

"I don't think that's likely, Janie," Aunt Cissie said as she got up to go into the kitchen. She looked at Janie with her gentle, blue eyes. "Mrs. Follett is my friend. We've always been good neighbours. They wouldn't send me letters like that, and they certainly wouldn't come into my house and disturb my things the way that — that *person* did."

But Janie was not so sure. She considered her list. Sometimes, in movies and television programmes she had seen, it was the nicest people, the least suspected, who were the guilty ones. And how quickly Mrs. Follett had volunteered to have her sons come over. What better opportunity could they have to do something in the house than if they were supposed to be staying there to guard it?

Janie put the Follett family third on her list of people who might have reasons to frighten Aunt Cissie.

Then Janie went back upstairs and took another piece of paper. She would keep a list of everyone who came to Dark Wood. Maybe the guilty person wasn't on her list of suspects at all. Maybe whatever reason it was that someone hated Aunt Cissie wasn't even known yet. But sooner or later maybe that person would come to the house, and then Janie would have his or her name.

Janie began her second list with Mrs. Follett, because she had been over first thing that morning. Later she would add the names of the Follett boys when they came to stay for the night.

She had two more names for her list when she looked down into the garden at the sound of a car motor and saw Mrs. Witticomb's black car stopping by the side porch.

She added to her list:

    Mrs. Witticomb
    Miss Perry

Her list was growing. Janie was sure that when it was complete it would have the name of the intruder and the letter-writer, if only she could be clever enough to figure it out.

More Names for the List

Janie's first sight of Mrs. Arnot, the antique dealer who wanted to buy Aunt Cissie's house, came that same afternoon. Mrs. Witticomb and Miss Perry stayed for lunch, and Janie helped Aunt Cissie prepare a bowl of tuna fish salad and sliced tomatoes. For dessert they served ice cream with Aunt Cissie's homemade caramel syrup.

Mrs. Witticomb ate two helpings of dessert, but Miss Perry did not have any at all. "I have to watch my figure," she explained.

After lunch, Janie sat on the top step of the porch. She was the first to see a car approaching up the road from the direction of town.

"Someone's coming, Aunt Cissie," Janie

called, as the car slowed and turned into Aunt Cissie's driveway.

"It's that Mrs. Arnot," Aunt Cissie said, peering at the car that had come to a halt at the edge of the driveway, its chrome trim flashing in the sunlight.

"What does she want now?" Mrs. Witticomb said. She had heard about Mrs. Arnot asking to buy the house.

As they watched, a tall, angular woman stepped out of the car and came striding toward the porch steps. She lifted her arm to shield her eyes from the sunlight until she came close enough to the house to be in the shade. Her hair was combed back tightly and twisted into a coil on the back of her neck, and she carried a large, shoulder-strap bag of dark leather.

Janie was disappointed. The words "antique dealer" brought to her mind the picture of a woman wearing ancient rings from China and ropes of precious beads and a fur coat in the winter-time. Nothing so plain as that knot of hair and those flat walking shoes.

But it was another name for her list of people who came to Dark Wood.

"Hello," Mrs. Arnot greeted Aunt Cissie as she neared the steps.

"Hello, Mrs. Arnot," Aunt Cissie said. She regarded the visitor cautiously.

"Mrs. Witticomb, Miss Perry." Mrs. Arnot nodded at the others, whom she knew slightly, and her gaze rested briefly on Janie. But she did not seem particularly interested in Janie and it was a fleeting glance. Janie could tell at once that Mrs. Arnot was one of those grown-ups to whom children did not really count as "people."

"I was just driving by and saw you sitting out here, so I thought I'd stop and see whether you've reconsidered my offer," Mrs. Arnot said. She directed her attention to Aunt Cissie, fastening her with a steady, persistent look. "After all, I've offered you a good price. You'd be wise to take it, I think."

Aunt Cissie was shaking her head. "I don't want to sell my house, Mrs. Arnot. I haven't changed my mind since you were here. I haven't been reconsidering your offer. I told you I wouldn't."

"People always reconsider offers where money is concerned," Mrs. Arnot said. "My business is based on that. People I sell to like to go home and sleep on it, as the saying goes, if they have some particularly large purchase in mind. People I buy from, I always give them time to consider my offers if they don't want to sell at first. I never rush people. That's bad business."

Aunt Cissie smiled faintly. Mrs. Arnot always made her feel weary, she was so intense.

"I never rush people," Mrs. Arnot repeated. Then she added, more slowly, "But I never give up, either."

"Give up on this," Mrs. Witticomb snapped. She had hoisted herself from the porch chair and stood towering at the top of the steps.

Miss Perry, seeing that Mrs. Witticomb was preparing to leave, had also risen. She held her handbag at her side and swung it idly by the strap. Janie was surprised to notice that she was smiling — but at what Janie could not tell.

There was a moment's silence as the people on the porch and Mrs. Arnot at the foot of the steps looked at each other. It was not a friendly silence. Janie drew closer to the porch railing and felt the hard edge of the wood against her back. It felt comforting in the silence to feel that secure, hard porch railing behind her.

At last Mrs. Arnot shrugged. "I'll be back again one of these days, Mrs. Mariott, in case you change your mind," she said. She started to turn away and then added, "No hard feelings," before she strode back to her car.

"Hmmp!" Mrs. Witticomb pronounced, as they all watched Mrs. Arnot get into her car and drive off.

"Now I hope that woman is not going to come around every week bothering me," Aunt Cissie fretted.

"Nonsense," Mrs. Witticomb declared sturdily. "She's just one of those headstrong people bent on getting her own way."

When Janie went upstairs to her bedroom, she got out her list of people who came to the house and added "Mrs. Arnot" in rather large letters. Later, when Dave and Jon Follett came to stay overnight, Janie put their names on the list, too.

The boys came just before dark. Janie knew them from summers before, and she had gone fishing with them a few times. Dave was eighteen and Jon was sixteen. They both had sandy hair and brown eyes, and they looked like farmer's sons in their blue jeans and plaid cotton shirts. They brought a plate of biscuits their mother had made for Aunt Cissie and Janie. But when Aunt Cissie poured glasses of milk for everybody, the boys ate up about half the biscuits themselves.

"I suppose boys never get filled up, do they?" Aunt Cissie said fondly.

"No, never," Dave said, winking at Janie.

Jon was too busy licking chocolate frosting from a fingertip to reply.

"Cat got your tongue?" Dave teased Janie.

Aunt Cissie sniffed, remembering her tomato-throwing, and said, "Please don't mention cats."

The boys had brought sleeping bags, ones they took when they went on overnight camping trips. They were going to put them on the parlour floor, although Aunt Cissie was afraid the floor would be too hard.

"I could open one of the other bedrooms," Aunt Cissie said. "The beds are still there, even though the rooms aren't used."

"That wouldn't be as good as our being right downstairs by the doors," Jon said. "Besides, we're not really going to sleep much. We're supposed to be keeping a lookout, remember?"

"I don't know how much sleeping I'll get done tonight myself," Aunt Cissie said with a sigh.

But she went to bed early, for the last two days had been a strain, to say the least. By ten o'clock the house was quiet, sitting in the warm summer darkness, with the sound of crickets the only thing to break the stillness.

Janie drew the sheet close up around her, even though the night was warm. Downstairs the two boys were keeping watch. They seemed nice enough, but how could she really be sure they weren't part of the plot to frighten Aunt Cissie? Jane remembered a film she had seen where a woman living alone carefully locked all her doors and windows because someone was trying to murder her, and then she found that she had locked the would-be murderer inside with her!

Janie hoped Aunt Cissie was not being protected by the very people who wanted to harm her.

The Phone Calls

For the rest of the week Jon and Dave Follett came over to Aunt Cissie's house at dusk and spent each night.

They kept their sleeping bags rolled up on Aunt Cissie's back porch during the day, and at night they took turns sleeping and keeping watch.

There was no further sign of an intruder, and there were no more mysterious letters in the post. But a sense of uneasiness hung over Dark Wood during the long, warm summer days and through the silent darkness of the nighttime.

It was the second week that the phone calls began — one evening after supper, before the Follett boys had arrived. Janie and Aunt

Cissie were in the kitchen washing the supper dishes when the first call came. As the phone rang, Aunt Cissie had just begun to dry her hands on a towel, and she said, "Would you answer that, Janie? My hands are still wet."

Janie went down the hall and answered the phone. "Hello," she said, but there was no answer. "Hello," she said again when she did not hear anyone on the line. There was only silence.

"Hello — hello —" Janie repeated.

At last she hung up the receiver.

"Who was that?" Aunt Cissie had come to the doorway.

"Nobody," said Janie. "Nobody answered."

Aunt Cissie did not say anything for a moment. Then she asked, "Did it sound as if someone was on the other end of the line, or was it just a dialling tone?"

"I think somebody was there, Aunt Cissie, only they didn't say anything. I said hello three or four times, but nobody answered —"

As Janie was speaking, the phone rang again. They both looked at it, and then at each other. Aunt Cissie nodded for Janie to answer.

Janie picked up the receiver cautiously. "Hello." There was silence again, and Janie shook her head to let Aunt Cissie know that no one was answering her.

Aunt Cissie motioned for Janie to go on, and Janie said "Hello" a second time.

This time there was an answer of a sort. A voice began to laugh softly on the other end of the line. It was a chilling sound, and Janie felt her skin prickle as she listened.

Aunt Cissie came and took the phone. "Hello, who is this —" she started to say. Then she stopped as she began to hear the laughing, too.

Aunt Cissie hung up the receiver abruptly. Her face was pale, but she tried to speak calmly. "Just a wrong number, I expect, Janie." But she knew, and Janie knew, that it wasn't a wrong number at all. The call was meant for Aunt Cissie. So was the laughter. Later, when Aunt Cissie spoke of the phone call to Chief Hadley, she said it was a "hating laugh."

After that the phone calls came two or three times a day. They came at different hours, without a pattern of any kind. Sometimes there was that awful laughter; and sometimes there was a whisper, a few words breathed softly through the phone. "I'm still watching you . . ." the voice said.

It was several days after the phone calls began when Janie realised that there were never any calls after dark, when the Follett boys were in the house. Whoever was making the calls seemed to know that Aunt Cissie and Janie would be more frightened if they were alone in the house when the calls came.

Or, Janie thought, maybe one, or both, of the Follett boys were making the calls themselves.

The thought startled Janie, but when she mentioned it, Aunt Cissie was quick to shake her head.

"It couldn't be the Follett boys, Janie. Why, that family is one of the nicest I've ever known. I'd trust any one of them with my life, if necessary."

"You would?" This seemed like an extreme measure to Janie.

"Yes, I would," Aunt Cissie answered emphatically. "Besides, Janie, it was a woman's voice."

Janie had to admit this was something to consider. "It could be somebody imitating a woman," she said to Aunt Cissie.

"It could be, I suppose," Aunt Cissie agreed doubtfully. "But whoever it is, I'm sure it's not one of the Folletts."

Janie did not really want to suspect the Follett boys. They had always been very nice to her in past summers. Jon had taken up woodcarving the year before and had made Janie a tiny wooden boat. She had painted it red, and Aunt Cissie had made a sail for it. Janie had it at home on her side board. This summer Jon said he would make her a cat, and she was going to paint it black . . . no, maybe grey or white would be better. A black cat did not seem very cheery.

Jon had already begun to make the cat. He brought the wood along when he came in the evenings, and he and Janie would sit at the kitchen table, and she would watch him as he worked. One night, as they sat there, they heard a noise in the cellar. Dave and Aunt Cissie had gone outside for a few minutes, and Jon and Janie were alone in the house.

"What was that?" Janie asked nervously.

Jon cocked his head to listen. The noise came again. It was definitely from the cellar. Something was bumping against something.

Jon put down the wooden cat and stood up. The cellar door was in the kitchen. He opened it and stood looking down into the darkness. Janie stayed right where she was. She didn't think she wanted to go down into that dark cellar to find out what was making the noise.

But Jon didn't seem frightened. He listened

a moment longer, and when the bumping sound came again, he started down the cellar stairs.

Janie got up then and went to the cellar door, peering timidly down into the gloom. Suddenly a light blinked on below as Jon pulled the light chain. She could see him standing there at the foot of the stairs looking around. Then he turned and called up to her. "It's only a window banging. I expect the latch came loose."

He disappeared from view, and she went down a few steps until she could see him again. He was dragging an old chair over toward one of the windows.

"Yes, I was right," he said. "Just a loose latch." He climbed on the chair, and Janie watched while he fastened the latch that had come loose. "Rather old and rusty," he said, brushing his hands. "That should hold it now."

Janie sat down on the bottom step.

"This really is an old cellar," Jon said. He scuffed his toe at the hard earth floor. Then he began to walk around looking at things, not touching anything at first, his hands in his pockets. Janie drew her knees up and huddled on the step. She was not really afraid, with

Jon there and the light on. But she never liked the idea that she might see a mouse in Aunt Cissie's cellar. After a few moments she got up and began to look around with Jon. They examined the labels on Aunt Cissie's preserve jars and poked through a wicker basket of garden tools and seed catalogues. In one corner there was an old roll-top desk with two drawers missing and a leg off. It was propped up with a box, on the outside of which Aunt Cissie had long ago written: *quilt scraps.*

There was the photograph of Cousin Emily propped in one shadowy corner. Her face loomed at Janie out of the darkness. For a moment, looking at it, Janie had an eerie feeling, as if Cousin Emily herself were there, watching Janie from that dim corner. It made her shiver.

Janie had had enough. The cellar was dark and unfriendly and full of things from years gone by that she did not like or understand. She wanted to get upstairs into the familiar, cosy rooms of Aunt Cissie's house — out of the cellar with Cousin Emily's picture watching her, and heaven knows how many spiders and things in hidden places.

Jon followed her up the stairs, pulling the light cord as he came. The cellar was thrown into blackness again, and Janie closed the door with relief. She decided she wasn't going down there again except in daytime, when light filtered across the floor from the cellar windows and it did not seem so frightening.

Yet she still seemed to feel Cousin Emily's eyes watching her from that dark corner.

An Unfriendly Neighbour

Janie wanted to put Mr. and Mrs. Johnson on her list of people who came to Dark Wood, but they never visited Aunt Cissie. Although their property adjoined hers and they were actually closer than the Follett family, Mrs. Johnson did not come visiting as Mrs. Follett did. And, of course, Mr. Johnson was usually angry at Aunt Cissie about something. It seemed that the Johnsons' cats were the only ones who came calling, even though Aunt Cissie did throw tomatoes at them.

By the end of the second week, Janie's list of people who had come to Dark Wood looked like this:

Wednesday: Mrs. Follett
              Mrs. Witticomb

	Miss Perry
	Mrs. Arnot
	Dave Follett
	Jon Follett
Thursday:	Mr. Coretti (the postman — who had come up to the house to leave a catalogue that would not fit in the postbox by the road)
	Mrs. Follett
	Dave and Jon Follett
Friday:	Chief Hadley
	Dave and Jon Follett
Saturday:	Mrs. Follett
	Mrs. Witticomb
	Miss Perry
	Sergeant Denton
	Dave and Jon Follett
Sunday:	Mr. Follett

Mr. Follett was a lanky, stoop-shouldered man who looked like his sons, with sandy hair and brown eyes. His skin was burned dark from working out of doors, and his eyes had wrinkles around them from squinting in the sunlight.

"You still make the best raisin biscuits I've ever eaten, Mrs. Mariott," he said, sitting at the kitchen table with his long legs sprawled out underneath, nearly across to the other side. Eating meals with him must be a problem for Mrs. Follett, Janie thought, if he stretched his legs underneath the table like that.

"I can't tell you what a help it's been having Dave and Jon stay with me these past nights," Aunt Cissie said. Her mind was not on raisin biscuits, even if she was being praised for them. She picked nervously at the throat of her flower-print dress.

"Glad to help all we can," Mr. Follett said.

Janie continued her list of visitors. The same names appeared over and over. Mrs. Follett. Dave and Jon. Chief Hadley. And then late one afternoon, Janie at last added the name:

Mr. Johnson

He came into the garden towards suppertime. Janie and Aunt Cissie had just come back from shopping and were unpacking groceries on the kitchen table. It was as though Mr. Johnson had waited to see Aunt Cissie's car in the drive and then came straight over. He had something on his mind, and he didn't waste any time getting to the point.

56

"Mrs. Mariott, I want to talk to you about that poplar tree the lightning hit last summer," he said through the kitchen screen door.

Aunt Cissie folded her arms and stood by the door, watching Mr. Johnson through the screen. Janie picked the stem from a strawberry she had just taken from the bag. She held the strawberry under the kitchen tap before putting it in her mouth. It was tart and rather hard, and she chewed on it with a sense of its bitterness while she listened to Mr. Johnson.

"Branches are going to come off that tree the first time we get a high wind blowing," Mr. Johnson complained. "It ought to come down. I've said so all along."

"But the tree's not dead, Mr. Johnson," Aunt Cissie protested. She tried to sound calm. "I know you've mentioned it before, but I hate to take down any tree if it's not dead."

"It's past it's life," Mr. Johnson said. "Poplar trees aren't good for too many years, and that one's dying. Those branches are brittle, and the tree ought to come down before somebody gets hurt. Some smaller branches have already fallen into my garden."

Aunt Cissie was taken aback to hear this. "I

am sorry about that, Mr. Johnson. I don't want anybody to get hurt, you know that."

"I thought you ought to know," he said. He had a big blue handkerchief in his pocket, and he took it out and wiped his forehead. It was a warm afternoon, and he was sweating from his walk across the sunny field.

"Would you like a drink of water, Mr. Johnson?" Aunt Cissie asked at last. Her tone said it was the least she could do, even if they weren't exactly best friends.

"I could use one," Mr. Johnson answered. He even sounded angry about that, Janie thought.

Aunt Cissie opened the screen door and Mr. Johnson came in.

"Janie, would you get a glass of water for Mr. Johnson, please?" Aunt Cissie said.

Janie got a glass from the cupboard and let the water run at the sink until it felt cold to her fingertips.

"Thank you, girl," Mr. Johnson said. He drank the glass of water with one long gulp and wiped the back of his hand across his mouth.

"I'll have another," he said, holding the glass out to Janie for a refill.

He certainly wasn't shy, Janie thought. Complaining about poor Aunt Cissie's poplar tree and drinking up all her water.

As Mr. Johnson left he said again, gruffly, "That tree's got to come down, Mrs. Mariott. No two ways about it. You know it as well as I do."

"I'll see what I can do," Aunt Cissie promised reluctantly. She knew Mrs. Johnson worked in her garden a good deal, and Aunt Cissie surely didn't want her to be hit by any falling poplar branches. It had been a trial to Aunt Cissie through all the years that the Johnson house and garden were so close to her own property.

As soon as Janie could get up to her room, she put Mr. Johnson's name on her list and sat studying it for a few minutes. She was not sure if she thought he was more suspicious than Mrs. Arnot — but he certainly wasn't very friendly.

As she came downstairs again, Janie heard the phone ringing and Aunt Cissie's steps going from the kitchen to the parlour to answer.

"Hello —" Aunt Cissie's voice stopped almost before she had finished saying the word. When Janie got to the parlour door, her aunt was standing with the phone in her hand, but not to her ear. Whatever the caller wanted to say had been said. Aunt Cissie's mouth was pinched, and her face was white.

"She said, 'I'll get my way,'" Aunt Cissie said to Janie. "And then that horrid laughing again."

They went back to the kitchen and started supper. But even making strawberry shortcake was no fun. And Janie noticed that Aunt Cissie hardly touched her supper at all.

In the Antique Shop

First the letters, then the house messed up, then the whispers and laughing on the phone. Each thing seemed to be harder for Aunt Cissie than the one before. And what would be next?

"I can't even eat any more," she said forlornly to Janie the next morning as they sat at the breakfast table. She looked at her plate with scrambled eggs and toast and marmalade, and she could not eat a bite.

Janie ate her breakfast slowly, not enjoying it much herself. But she thought if she said anything about not feeling like eating, Aunt Cissie might say that Janie ought to go home. So Janie pretended that she didn't feel too bad. She even tried to hum to herself as she cleared off the breakfast dishes.

All morning she watched Aunt Cissie pick up and discard one thing after another. She got out her knitting and tried to knit, but gave that up. She said she was going to write some letters, but Janie saw that she only sat at her desk twiddling her pen and staring at the paper without writing anything. By lunchtime Aunt Cissie had grown so oppressed and restless that Janie was not surprised to hear her say, "I've got to get out of this house for a while, Janie. After lunch we'll drive into town. I've been meaning to get some new bedroom slippers."

As always now, whenever they went out for any reason, Aunt Cissie and Janie made sure that both the front and back doors were securely locked.

"A case of closing the stable door after the horse is gone, I'm afraid," Aunt Cissie muttered under her breath. She put on her hat and picked up her handbag.

The phone rang just as they closed the front door behind them. From the porch they could hear its persistent shrill.

"Never mind," Aunt Cissie said, turning away from the door and starting down the steps. "Let it ring."

Janie clattered down the steps close behind

Aunt Cissie. It was certainly the strangest summer she had ever spent at Dark Wood.

When they came out of the shoe shop, with Aunt Cissie's new bedroom slippers in a bright red shoe box, Janie saw a sign on a shop across the street: ARNOT'S ANTIQUES — FINEST IN FAIRFIELD.

"Look, there's Mrs. Arnot's shop," she said, tugging at Aunt Cissie's sleeve. "Can we go over? I've never been in an antique shop."

Aunt Cissie hesitated and looked across the street, frowning. As they watched, a man and woman came along and went into the shop.

"I'm not too eager to see that Mrs. Arnot," Aunt Cissie said slowly. "I don't want her to start bothering me again about selling Dark Wood."

But Janie was curious to see the shop — and perhaps, if she would have admitted it, curious to see Mrs. Arnot again. She looked up at Aunt Cissie hopefully. "Maybe she won't say anything about it when she has customers," she urged Aunt Cissie.

Aunt Cissie still hesitated, but at last she smiled and said, "Oh, all right. I suppose I can stand Mrs. Arnot for a few minutes if you really want to see the shop."

They went across the street and stopped to

look in the window. There were small things on display — copper trays and glass vases and several pewter pitchers. Through the window Janie could see pieces of furniture.

"Well we'd better go in if we're going," Aunt Cissie said.

Inside, the shop seemed very dim as they came in from the bright sunlight. The man and woman who had entered a few minutes before were standing near the back examining a table. Mrs. Arnot stood beside them. She glanced over her shoulder at Aunt Cissie and Janie when she heard the door opening. If Mrs. Arnot was surprised to see Aunt Cissie, she did not show it.

There was a soft gleam of wood and brass to the shop interior, and Janie was pleased with the many things that hung upon the walls: old lanterns and picture frames and whatnot shelves with figurines. She began to walk around carefully between the pieces of furniture, not touching anything. She thought that antiques must be fragile if they were so old, and she was afraid they might fall apart in her fingers.

Soon, Mrs. Arnot came toward Janie and Aunt Cissie. She was wearing the same sturdy shoes, and had the same knot of hair at the back of her neck.

"Janie's never been in an antique store," Aunt Cissie explained quickly. "We were just passing, and I said she could come in and look around for a few minutes." She wanted Mrs. Arnot to understand right away that her arrival at the store had nothing to do with selling Dark Wood.

"I see." Mrs. Arnot gave Janie a brief nod. "Look round as much as you like."

After a few minutes, Aunt Cissie sat down on a chair and rested her feet while Janie looked round the shop. She came across a table where pieces of old jewellery were on display in a long glass-topped box. She was resting her elbows on the table, her long fair hair sweeping down on both sides of her face, when she became aware that Mrs. Arnot was standing beside her. Guiltily, Janie straightened up. She should not have been leaning against the table on her elbows. But Mrs. Arnot did not mention that.

"Isn't that old jewellery pretty?" she said. "Here's something you might like." She opened a box and took out a small gold ring with a blue stone.

"This was a child's ring. Try it on," she suggested.

Janie slipped it on her little finger, but it was too loose. It fitted quite well on the next finger, and she turned her hand in different positions admiring the ring.

"And here's a pretty locket," Mrs. Arnot said. She held up a tiny gold locket for Janie to see. "This was a baby's locket, and here's another pretty one, but it's not a child's." She held a locket with a circle of tiny pearls on the front.

"They're all so pretty," Janie told her.

Mrs. Arnot stayed beside Janie and got interested herself in trying to open the locket with the pearls. But it would not open. "The catch has been bent out of shape, I'm afraid," she said at last. Then she put the locket down and went to talk to a customer.

Janie put the locket back carefully with the other jewellery and tried on another ring. It was fun to think that years and years ago someone had worn these rings and lockets.

While Mrs. Arnot was busy talking to the customer, Aunt Cissie motioned to Janie to come along quickly so they could slip out before Mrs. Arnot could bother Aunt Cissie about selling her house.

They stopped at the Fairfield Bakery and Aunt Cissie bought a coconut cake to give to

Dave and Jon when they came that night to guard Dark Wood.

But at last there were no more errands to do, nothing to keep them from going home. Aunt Cissie sighed to herself as they got in the car and started back to the house.

An Afternoon with
Mrs. Witticomb

That night Mrs. Witticomb called and invited Aunt Cissie and Janie to go for a drive the next day.

"You should get out of the house more often," Mrs. Witticomb said.

"I do get out," Aunt Cissie told her. "Janie and I went shopping in town twice this week."

"Shopping trips are not outings in my book," Mrs. Witticomb objected. "We'll go for a drive and stop back here at my house. I'll get some of those éclairs Janie likes so much."

"All right," Aunt Cissie agreed.

"Miss Perry and I will be round about one o'clock tomorrow," Mrs. Witticomb said.

Dave and Jon Follett had already arrived for the night. When Aunt Cissie went to tell

Janie what Mrs. Witticomb had suggested, the boys were sitting at the dining room table playing Monopoly with Janie.

Aunt Cissie sat down at the table and looked at the Monopoly board without really seeing it. "I can't thank you boys enough for coming like this every night," she said.

"We could thank them with some coconut cake," Janie reminded Aunt Cissie. She nodded toward the kitchen where Aunt Cissie had set out the cake they had bought that afternoon.

"Now my mind's going," Aunt Cissie muttered to herself. She started to get up.

"I'll do it," Janie said. She wanted to be very helpful and efficient, because every day she worried that Aunt Cissie would send her home.

"No, thank you, dear," said Aunt Cissie. And she brought in the cake.

The next day was hot. The hottest day since Janie had arrived. Aunt Cissie kept dabbing at her face with her handkerchief as she got ready to go out with Mrs. Witticomb. Even Janie wiggled her toes in her shoes and wished she could go barefoot.

When Mrs. Witticomb and Miss Perry arrived, they came in the house, and Miss Perry said she thought Mrs. Witticomb would like some ice water before they went on for their drive. Miss Perry herself accepted Aunt Cissie's offer of ice tea to drink. Half a pot of tea was left from lunch, and Miss Perry came out to the kitchen with Janie and helped her get out glasses and spoons.

It was too hot to really enjoy a drive. They had not gone far when Mrs. Witticomb said she thought they would be more comfortable if they went back to her house.

Miss Perry had some errands to do, but Aunt Cissie and Janie stayed at Mrs. Witticomb's house until after four o'clock, eating the chocolate éclairs that Janie was so fond of.

"How many would you eat, if you could have all you wanted?" Mrs. Witticomb said.

"About a hundred," Janie answered.

"*Hmmp.*" Mrs. Witticomb leaned back into her chair and closed her eyes and fanned herself.

Aunt Cissie stared unhappily out of the window. Why am I so fearful sometimes? she thought to herself. Mrs. Witticomb wouldn't be frightened by four scrawly letters and a few phone calls. Angry perhaps and determined to find out who had done it. But not frightened.

Aunt Cissie shivered suddenly and wondered

if everything was all right at Dark Wood. When she saw Miss Perry returning from her errands, she stood up quickly. "We've got to get back now, Janie — it's late."

Mrs. Witticomb opened one eye and looked at the clock on the wall. "Stay a little longer," she said.

But Aunt Cissie was not to be persuaded. She wanted to get home.

More Trouble

It seemed that Miss Perry could not drive fast enough for Aunt Cissie as they started home. The countryside flashed by, but Aunt Cissie's need to hurry only increased. When they finally turned on to Oak Road, even Janie felt that they had been driving forever.

"Here you are, Mrs. Mariott," Miss Perry said as they swung into Aunt Cissie's drive. "Home safe and sound."

Janie ran ahead, around the side of the house toward the back porch. The kitchen door was open. They had left it locked, but now she could see through the screen into the kitchen!

Slowly, Janie pulled open the screen door. Everything in the kitchen looked just as they had left it. But something was wrong. A queer, waiting silence filled the room.

Janie took a few steps into the room, acting braver than she felt. Then she saw the pantry door. It stood open, and for a moment she hesitated, holding her breath. But there was not a sound. Behind her, outside in the garden, she could hear Miss Perry's voice as she came around the corner of the house with Aunt Cissie. "Your flower garden is lovely this summer, Mrs. Mariott," she was saying.

Janie took a few more steps and peered cautiously around the half-open door into the pantry.

Someone or something had been in there. The flour bag was slit and so was the box of sugar. Piles of spilled flour and sugar had trickled to the floor. A bag of apples had been emptied, and a loaf of bread was scattered around. Cans of food had been knocked from the shelves.

Suddenly, Janie was aware that Aunt Cissie and Miss Perry were standing behind her. She realised it first when she heard Aunt Cissie's faint cry of disbelief at what she saw as she gazed over Janie's shoulder.

"Oh — Mrs. Mariott — what's happened?" Miss Perry was the first one able to speak.

"Oh — oh —" Aunt Cissie sank into a chair, her hands fluttering in the air.

It looked as though some animal had been rampaging through the food. But no animal had slit open the flour bag and the box of sugar. Jon Follett's woodcarving knife had been driven upright into one of the wooden shelves over the flour bag. The blade glistened in the light.

A Frightening Night

Despite the knife, Aunt Cissie refused to believe that Jon Follett had caused the damage in her pantry.

Even Janie could not think that he would have done such a thing. Besides, why would he leave his knife for everyone to see? It didn't make sense.

The Folletts came over at once. When Jon explained that he had forgotten his knife the evening before, everyone felt that he was telling the truth. He was just as amazed as everyone else as he looked at the spilled and scattered food.

"Of course you didn't do it, Jon," Aunt Cissie said tearfully. "Someone just used your knife. If it hadn't been here, they would have taken one of my kitchen knives, I'm sure."

"Yes," Mr. Follett said, "that's probably just what happened." Then he drew Aunt Cissie aside and said that he would come and stay at night instead of the boys. "Not that they can't take care of things," he said, "but I want to be on hand myself if anything else happens. I should have been here all along."

"You're all so kind," Aunt Cissie murmured. She dabbed at her eyes with a handkerchief and watched as Janie and Jon and Dave began to clean up the mess in the pantry.

"What are things coming to? What are things coming to?" Aunt Cissie said over and over to herself. But she could not find the answer.

It was surely the strangest summer Janie had ever spent at Dark Wood. But now it was drawing to an end. School would soon be starting. Her three weeks with Aunt Cissie were ending, and there might never be another summer at Aunt Cissie's house.

"I don't think I can stay here much longer, Janie," Aunt Cissie said on the night after they had found the pantry ransacked.

Janie did not know what to say. Her eyes filled with tears as she looked at dear Aunt Cissie sitting on the edge of the bed in her faded blue dressing gown, her hands clutched together forlornly.

"I never thought I could leave here, Janie," she said, "but I can't live like this — police in and out, imposing on neighbours to stay overnight with me. I could get a watchdog — Chief Hadley suggested that. But I can't live in fear like this all the time. I can't be wondering every time I go out of my house what I'm going to find when I come back." She shook her head sadly. "Maybe I ought to sell the Folletts the land that they want, and cut down the tree that bothers Mr. Johnson, and then sell the house to Mrs. Arnot."

"But where would you go?" Janie knew that Aunt Cissie had always said she would not ever want to live anywhere else but the old country house she loved so well.

"I don't know." Aunt Cissie shook her head. "I just don't know. . . . Oh, I wish I were braver, Janie."

It made Janie feel queer as she sat in bed, listening to Aunt Cissie talking about leaving Dark Wood.

The next day, as though she had sensed a change in the wind, Mrs. Arnot came driving out from town to ask Aunt Cissie if she had reconsidered her offer.

"As a matter of fact," Aunt Cissie answered slowly, "I have been thinking about your offer, Mrs. Arnot. I never thought I could bring myself to think of selling my father's house, but I'm not so sure now."

Mrs. Arnot's eyes gleamed with satisfaction. Janie was watching her from the corner of the parlour, and she could almost hear Mrs. Arnot thinking "I told you so."

"That's interesting news, Mrs. Mariott," Mrs. Arnot said briskly. "This room would be the main salesroom, and I could display Early American paintings and wall decorations in the hallway leading back to the kitchen. The kitchen would be ideal for old pewter and rocking chairs, that sort of thing—"

She was striding about in her sturdy shoes, pushing open doors here and there and mentally arranging her stock of antiques in various places through the house.

"I haven't said for sure yet," Aunt Cissie reminded Mrs. Arnot faintly. But Mrs. Arnot hardly heard. "Don't get your hopes too high," Aunt Cissie added.

Mrs. Arnot laughed rather sternly. "I haven't succeeded in my business by high hopes," she said.

Aunt Cissie and Janie watched the antique

dealer's car dwindling in the distance of the road. "I feel as though a lorry has run over me when she talks," Aunt Cissie said.

Janie leaned close to her and patted her arm comfortingly. "Maybe you won't have to sell your house, Aunt Cissie."

But Aunt Cissie continued to gaze down the road, even though Mrs. Arnot's car was out of sight. "I've lived here a good many years, Janie. I don't want to go now."

"Then don't go. Don't let anybody frighten you away." Janie's face was sober, her forehead lined with a frown of determination.

Later that evening, as dusk settled around Dark Wood, Aunt Cissie began to look through the kitchen window toward the Follett's house. Mr. Follett usually came across the back field. But tonight he did not come.

The countryside was rapidly growing dark. Already the woods across the road were lost in gloom, and cars speeding by with bright headlights seemed to make the darkness blacker by contrast. Before long it would be completely dark.

"Why don't we phone him?" Janie suggested.

"I hate to bother him if he's only been delayed a bit," Aunt Cissie said. "They've been so good about coming to stay with us all these nights. I hate to call up the first time he's a little late."

Together Janie and Aunt Cissie sat on the back porch steps and watched the darkness fall over the countryside. Fireflies lit up in the shadows, and crickets began to chirp. It was the first night since the house had been broken into that Aunt Cissie and Janie had been alone in the evening.

At last Aunt Cissie stood up from the steps slowly and stiffly. "I believe I will call and see if anything's wrong at their house," she said. "Something must have happened for Mr. Follett not to come or call or *anything*."

The house was dark inside except for the light in the kitchen. Janie did not like going along the hall towards the dim parlour. Dark Wood seemed very still and somehow dangerous to Janie. She kept close to Aunt Cissie.

In the parlour Aunt Cissie reached out for the lamp that was on the table beside the telephone. As the light clicked on, Aunt Cissie and Janie drew back in horror.

Curled on the telephone table was a long black snake. As the light went on, it stirred and began to uncurl against the telephone.

Janie was too frightened to move. For a

long, horrible moment, she and Aunt Cissie stood breathless. She could feel the hair rise along her arms as the snake coiled around the base of the lamp on the telephone table.

Then, suddenly, the whole room was plunged into darkness. Janie saw that the hall leading back to the kitchen was in total darkness, too. No lamplight shone from the open kitchen door. A minute before they had followed its beam down the hallway to the parlour. Now every light in the house was out. They were alone in the room with the snake — and they could no longer see where it was in the darkness.

A sound came from the telephone table as the snake slid against something. Perhaps at this moment it was slithering across the carpet toward their feet. Janie drew back in fright and fell over a footstool.

Aunt Cissie cried out. And then behind them they heard the parlour door close and a key turning in the lock.

They were cut off in a dark room, with only the sound of the snake moving.

A Time for Bravery

"Janie — Janie, are you hurt?"

Aunt Cissie groped in the darkness to help her. Janie felt Aunt Cissie's hand on her arm, fumbling and unsteady, but there to help.

Janie scrambled up from the floor, biting her lip and feeling tears rise in her eyes. She had hit her knee sharply on the leg of the footstool as she fell.

"Let's get back towards the door," Aunt Cissie gasped in a frightened whisper. Clinging to each other, they backed away from the telephone table toward the locked door. There was another bumping sound from the snake on the table, and then a loud noise as the lamp fell over and crashed to the floor.

"Oh, Janie — what will we do?"

They could not telephone for help because the snake was still on the table by the phone. In the light they would not have dared, much less now in the darkness.

"I could go out through a window and run to the Folletts' for help," Janie whispered.

"I can't stay here alone with that snake in the room —" Aunt Cissie's arms tightened around Janie's shoulders to hold her there.

"Yes, you can," Janie said. "I'll run as fast as I can —"

"No, no." Aunt Cissie was trembling more than ever now at the thought of Janie leaving her, even to get help. "Oh, why am I always so afraid? Janie, I want to be brave —"

"You *are* brave, Aunt Cissie," said Janie, who did not feel very brave herself. "You can stay here and I'll run for help, and we'll find out who's trying to scare you away. Oh, don't let them, Aunt Cissie — don't let anybody scare you away — please."

There was silence for a moment. Janie felt the old woman's arms clutching her, and then suddenly she felt them begin to grow less tight, less rigid in their hold. Faltering still, Aunt Cissie said, "All right, Janie. If I'm ever going to be brave, I suppose this is the time for it. I — I won't be frightened away." She paused, and then continued more steadily. "You go. Can you find your way in the dark?"

"Yes," Janie whispered, although the very question had occurred to her with a less reassuring answer in her own heart. How could she drop from the window into dark bushes and find her way at night across the fields to the Folletts' house? Whoever was trying to hurt Aunt Cissie might be anywhere outside in the darkness, and she would never see until it was too late. . . . But there did not seem to be anything else to do.

There was one parlour window that had no summer screen. The lock stuck under Janie's fingers. At last, with a desperate yank, she forced it around. The window, creaking with protest as both Janie and Aunt Cissie pushed at it, opened enough for Janie to fit through. For a moment Janie thought of suggesting that Aunt Cissie climb over the sill and escape from the snake, too. But the window opening was not large enough for Aunt Cissie, and the drop to the ground below was surely too much for anyone her age.

Janie's eyes were beginning to grow accustomed to the darkness. She wriggled over the windowsill without stopping to think what — or who — might be waiting for her outside in the dark night. If she stopped to think, perhaps she would not go. Behind her in the room there was another sound in the dark, and Janie felt Aunt Cissie's hand stiffen on her arm.

But Aunt Cissie did not waver in her decision. "Go on, Janie — go on —"

Janie dropped to the ground. "Are you all right?" Aunt Cissie whipered, trying to see down to where Janie was.

The bushes scratched against Janie's bare legs. She could see Aunt Cissie's dark form outlined above her in the window frame.

"I'm fine," she said. And then she began to run! Around the side of the house she fled and across the garden toward the pathway that led to the fields.

Then suddenly the driveway blazed with car headlights, and Janie heard a car door opening. She ran toward the lights gasping and tearful. Someone had come! She would not have to run through the dark fields for help — it had come to her.

It was Mrs. Witticomb's car. Janie ran

straight into Miss Perry as she stepped from the car and started to say, "Why, hello there, Janie —" Her words were interrupted by Janie's cries as she ran into her arms.

A Call to Mr. Follett

Whoever had put the snake in Aunt Cissie's house, whoever had cut off the electricity, whoever had locked Aunt Cissie and Janie in the parlour, was gone. Miss Perry got a torch from the car and hurried into the house with Janie through the unlocked kitchen door. There was not a sight or sound of anybody.

Miss Perry could not open the parlour door, but she ran upstairs to Aunt Cissie's bedroom where Janie said there was another phone. There were no lights working upstairs either, and Janie held the torch while Miss Perry dialed for the police. Then they went back downstairs and outside to the parlour window.

"Mrs. Mariott, we've notified the police," Miss Perry called through the window. She handed the torch up to Aunt Cissie, who held it in front of herself protectingly. Although she could not see where the snake was now, at least she could reassure herself that it was not close to her. She moved the beam of light slowly back and forth in front of her along the carpet. There was no sign of the snake. It could be anywhere in the room by this time, behind any piece of furniture. All Aunt Cissie wanted to know was that it was not sliding across the floor towards her.

"I was driving by," Miss Perry explained, "and I thought it was strange that the house should be all dark this early in the evening. So I thought I'd stop and see if everything was all right."

Chief Hadley's car was pulling into the driveway. Janie watched as the car came up the road and turned in, headlights sweeping the drive, glinting on Mrs. Witticomb's car parked at the side. Everything was going to be all right now, Janie thought: Chief Hadley had come. She was even glad to see Sergeant Denton. When he forced the lock and opened the parlour door for Aunt Cissie, Janie even forgave him for teasing Aunt Cissie about throwing tomatoes at cats. And she was sure Aunt Cissie forgave him, too.

It did not take Sergeant Denton long to round up the snake — a harmless one, but certainly large and wicked-looking enough to startle anyone. Chief Hadley had the lights back on almost at once. A switch in the cellar had been pulled to shut off the electricity, and it was a simple matter to turn it on again.

When Aunt Cissie and Janie told their story, Chief Hadley was also puzzled about why Mr. Follett had not come at his usual time and had not, in fact, arrived at all.

"What's his number?" Chief Hadley asked.

"Six-four-two," Aunt Cissie said. She was sitting in her rocker, an expression on her face that Janie had not seen before. It was a pale but triumphant look. Aunt Cissie had been frightened and yet she had let Janie go to get help. She had decided not to sell her home, not to be frightened away. She had decided this while she waited alone in the dark room with the snake.

"Hello — Follett? This is Chief Hadley. I'm here at Mrs. Mariott's house —" Mr. Follett interrupted. Chief Hadley listened a moment and then said, "Yes, there was some trouble. When you were late Mrs. Mariott wondered why and started to call you . . . What? What did you say? . . . Called *you*?" Chief Hadley listened to whatever Mr. Follett was saying and nodded.

Everyone waited curiously, and at last Chief Hadley said, "I think I'm beginning to understand. All right, I'll talk to you later."

Chief Hadley hung up the phone and stood for a moment staring down at it thoughtfully. Then he turned to face Aunt Cissie.

"Mr. Follett didn't come over this evening because he says you called him at about six o'clock and said he needn't come tonight, that I was sending Sergeant Denton to stay."

"Why — why —" Aunt Cissie stared at Chief Hadley in confusion.

"You didn't call him?"

"No, of course I didn't call him," Aunt Cissie said. "Why would I do that? I wondered why he wasn't here, and Janie and I came in to call him and found the snake, just as I told you."

Chief Hadley nodded. "The caller must have been imitating you."

Aunt Cissie clasped her hands and rocked back and forth in her chair.

"So, naturally, Follett thought the police were taking over for the night," Chief Hadley continued. "He says he watched television a while and then went to bed early."

Chief Hadley continued to look thoughtful. Janie wondered if he thought Mr. Follett had really watched television and gone to bed early. Or did he think Mr. Follett came to Aunt Cissie's house after all, put the snake in the parlour, turned off the electricity, and then went home again through the dark fields before Miss Perry arrived?

In Aunt Cissie's Room

Miss Perry was soon on her way again, urging Aunt Cissie to let Mrs. Witticomb know if there was anything they could do to help. Chief Hadley stayed a while talking to Aunt Cissie in the parlour. Janie followed Sergeant Denton in a thorough search of the house, to be sure there were no more snakes or other unpleasant surprises in any of the rooms.

It was comforting to Janie to walk beside the sergeant. The house did not seem so frightening now that he had come.

It was nearly ten o'clock when Chief Hadley started over to the Follett house to talk with Mr. Follett. Sergeant Denton was assigned to watch Aunt Cissie's house for the night, and

Aunt Cissie and Janie went upstairs to get ready for bed.

"Would you like to sleep with me tonight, Janie?" Aunt Cissie said impulsively, hesitating in the doorway of her bedroom. A lamp Sergeant Denton had turned on to search her room earlier in the evening cast a warm glow across the rose-coloured rug and white bedspread. Folded at the foot of the bed was a green and blue quilt that Aunt Cissie had bought at a quilt sale several summers before. Janie remembered it. It was the first summer she had started coming to visit Aunt Cissie, the first quilt sale she had ever gone to.

Janie usually slept with Aunt Cissie once or twice each summer, just for fun. Aunt Cissie's bed was a special treat for her. It was very high off the floor, with four tall posters and two great pillows. The bed was as old as the house itself, Aunt Cissie had told Janie. Soon the bed would be old enough to be an antique that Mrs. Arnot would no doubt like to have.

"You aren't too big to think it's fun to sleep in my funny old bed, are you, Janie?" Aunt Cissie asked. "In a few days you'll be going home again."

"Oh, no — I'd like to," Janie agreed. It was always fun to climb into the bed and stare at the designs carved on the tops of the old posters. And tonight especially she did not want to sleep alone.

It did not take Janie long to wash and get into her pyjamas. When she came back, Aunt Cissie had not made any move toward getting ready for bed herself. She was sitting in a chair by a small desk at one side of the room, her hands folded in her lap, her eyes staring at the desk without really seeing it.

Janie waited a moment. The evening had turned chilly, and her bare feet felt almost cold on the hardwood floor. She wondered if Aunt Cissie was brooding about the snake that had been downstairs.

"What are you thinking about?" Janie asked softly. Aunt Cissie looked around at her and almost, for a moment, did not seem to see Janie either.

"Why, I was just thinking about something Chief Hadley asked me that first day we went to his office. He asked me who might hate me or want to harm or frighten me —"

Janie nodded. She remembered well. Hadn't she herself made a list of the suspects?

"I've thought of someone else," Aunt Cissie said slowly.

Janie felt her breath draw in sharply. "Who?" she asked, leaning forward to hear Aunt Cissie's low voice. "Who did you think of?"

"My cousin Emily," Aunt Cissie said. "It's strange, isn't it, that I should think of her now, when I haven't thought of her much at all in years and years."

"But she's been gone such a long time." Janie was disappointed. She had supposed Aunt Cissie had thought of someone living right now in town, not a cousin who had lived with Aunt Cissie when they were growing up. She would be an old lady now, older even than Aunt Cissie.

"I don't suppose it could mean anything now, but Cousin Emily hated me very much when she left here," Aunt Cissie said regretfully. "She was the only person whom I ever felt did hate me, until now. Now someone else hates me, and maybe that's what finally made me think of Emily. It's an awful thing to feel that someone hates you, Janie." Aunt Cissie shook her head.

"Emily was a strange girl," Aunt Cissie continued, choosing her words carefully. "She was nice to me sometimes, but she always felt resentful that it was *my* mother and father, and *my* house — and she was only the orphan child taken in, so to speak.

"My mother and father were very kind to her and treated us like two sisters. But, of course, when my father died he left the house to me, and Emily was very hurt about that." Aunt Cissie closed her eyes, as though to see better some distant scene in her mind's eye.

"I told Emily she would be welcome to stay on with me as long as she wished. But she felt very bitter that my father had left her nothing. I suppose since my parents had treated her like a child of their own in so many ways, she had thought she would share in any inheritance. And I think it might really have been fairer if she had. I told her that Dark Wood was still her home. But she was too angry to stay, and I knew she hated me. Not many weeks after my father died, she left without a word, and I've never seen her since."

"How old was she?" Janie had listened to the story with wide eyes.

"Let me think." Aunt Cissie counted back over the years. "I was nineteen when my father died, and Emily was three years older."

"And you never heard anything more from her?"

"I never saw her again, but I did hear of her

now and then the first few years after she left. She wrote occasionally to a girl who had been a school friend while she lived here. The friend brought the letters to show me because she knew I was concerned about Emily. You see, she had no money to speak of when she left, and I wasn't sure how she was supporting herself.

"The first letter she wrote to her friend was angry and full of hatred. Emily said she was working in Chicago. She said she had faced the fact that she would have to work to take care of herself because *she* had no father to leave her a house and money."

"Did your father leave you a lot of money?" Janie asked with surprise. She had never thought of Aunt Cissie as being rich. Ever since Janie had known her, Aunt Cissie's living style had seemed very simple. And there was nothing extravagant or fancy about Dark Wood.

"Enough to live on for the rest of my life," Aunt Cissie said. "It was a trust fund, from which I draw a certain amount each year. Even today, with the many rises in costs, I can still get by. It meant I would never have to work, as Cousin Emily did. I imagine as she went about her duties as a maid in someone else's house, she grew more and more bitter to think that I was taken care of for the rest of my life."

Aunt Cissie was silent for a moment. Her fingers absently caressed the edge of the desk, in the room that was still so much like it had been so many years ago.

"It was fortunate for me, of course," she said at last. "I was married only a few years before my husband died. And he was an impractical man who saved little, I'm afraid." Aunt Cissie smiled gently. "Dear Sam. He was kind and generous, and completely unwise in handling money. But I had my father's trust money, had it then and have it still, for as long as I live."

"Did Cousin Emily ever marry?" Janie asked.

"Yes, that was the last word I ever had of her. She wrote to her friend again, saying she left her job and she was getting married. That was the last anyone heard from her."

Aunt Cissie sighed. "I tried to contact Emily, but my letters came back stamped 'return to sender,' and I never knew what her married name was. I always somehow wanted to make it up to her for what she felt was the injustice of my father's will. For some years afterwards I kept thinking she would come back one day, if not to see me, perhaps to see her school friend. But she never did. Years and years went by, and finally I stopped thinking she would ever return. I wouldn't have thought of her now if it wasn't that Chief Hadley asked me about anyone who might hate me."

Janie was silent. Cousin Emily didn't seem to have any connection with the things that had been happening to Aunt Cissie.

Aunt Cissie told Janie to get into bed and try to sleep. "Look how late it is," Aunt Cissie chided herself. "I'm sure your mother wouldn't approve of your being up so late, or being in the middle of all this confusion."

"I don't mind," Janie said, snuggling down in the bed. "I'm not tired."

Aunt Cissie smiled knowingly. "I'm going to sit up a bit. Now you get to sleep."

Janie lay in the softness of the pillows and freshly laundered sheets. Through half-closed eyes she could see Aunt Cissie sitting in the chair by the desk, her head resting against the high back of the chair, her eyes fixed absently on the darkness beyond the window. Was she still thinking back to girlhood days? Janie wondered. Feeling Cousin Emily's hatred sweep over her again when she thought she had forgotten it after all these years?

Janie felt very far from the solution to the mystery.

Janie's Discovery

Janie started to doze. Aunt Cissie's room began to grow bigger and bigger around her, wavering with lamplight and shadows and the great black square of darkness that was the window.

And then suddenly Janie was wide-awake. Something had woken her as she had been sleepily thinking over the rapid and frightening events of the evening.

Cousin Emily. Janie could see the brooding eyes of the photograph in the cellar . . . the severe pulled-back hairstyle, the old-fashioned puffed sleeves of the dress . . . and hanging around Cousin Emily's neck was a locket . . . a locket with a circle of tiny pearls on the front . . . the locket at Mrs. Arnot's antique shop . . .

101

Janie sat up abruptly. The covers slid forward. Aunt Cissie looked over and said, "What is it, dear?"

"Aunt Cissie, that locket Cousin Emily is wearing in the picture in the cellar — I saw it when we were at the antique shop!"

Aunt Cissie did not grasp what Janie was saying. Her thoughts had been so far away. "The antique shop?" she repeated vaguely.

"Yes — yes —" Janie was so excited now, she pushed off the rest of the covers and put her feet over the edge of the bed. When she stepped off the rug, the floor was cool against her bare feet.

"Cousin Emily's locket, the one in the picture — Mrs. Arnot has it at her shop."

"But — but — why, how could she have Emily's locket?" Aunt Cissie was still confused. She opened her arms. "You've been having a dream, Janie," she said tenderly. "All this excitement, and being up so late —"

"No, no," Janie insisted, shaking her head. "It's the same locket. I know it is. I remember it specially because I tried to open it. It was stuck, and Mrs. Arnot tried to get it open but she couldn't. And then I tried."

"But what has that got to do with my cousin Emily?"

"I didn't recognise it then, but I remember it now," Janie went on eagerly. "It's the same locket as in that picture of Cousin Emily in the cellar. Cousin Emily's come back — she *is* the one who hates you after all."

"That's impossible," Aunt Cissie stammered. "Emily's been gone for years and years."

"But Mrs. Arnot has her locket. I know it's the same one." Janie was beginning to feel frantic because she could not make Aunt Cissie understand. "Let's go downstairs into the cellar. I'll show you."

Aunt Cissie allowed herself to be drawn up from her chair. Janie didn't even stop to put her dressing gown on, but pulled Aunt Cissie along after her down the landing, down the stairs, and into the kitchen.

Sergeant Denton heard them coming down. "Everything all right?" he asked, sticking his head out of the parlour where he had been sitting.

"Yes, yes — we're just going down to the cellar for a moment," Aunt Cissie mumbled. Janie did not even glance in Sergeant Denton's direction. She held Aunt Cissie's hand and opened the door that led down into the cellar. She hoped there were no mice or spiders around, but she could not stop now.

Aunt Cissie went down first, holding the handrail firmly, although she surely knew those old cellar steps well enough to go up and down them blindfolded. Janie came close behind and felt the rush of relief that accompanied Aunt Cissie's pull on the light cord by the stairs.

"It's over here," Janie said. She remembered exactly where she had seen the picture when she was down in the cellar with Jon. The picture was in the same spot, beside the roll-top desk, propped against the wall in the shadows. Aunt Cissie drew it out into a better light, rubbing across the dusty glass with the edge of her skirt. Clearly discernible on Cousin Emily's dress hung a locket on a chain. A circle of pearls decorated the front of the locket, just like the one Janie had seen at Mrs. Arnot's antique shop.

"It's the same one, Aunt Cissie, I'm sure," Janie whispered with excitement.

Aunt Cissie made Janie look as closely as she could at the picture. "I want you to be sure, Janie," Aunt Cissie said. "Look carefully."

"I am," Janie said. "And it's the same one. I know it is, Aunt Cissie. It's the same one — it really is."

A Trip to Town

Janie thought she would never be able to get to sleep that night. She was so anxious for morning to come and for Aunt Cissie to call Mrs. Arnot.

When morning did come and Aunt Cissie was ready to telephone, Janie stood beside her, first on one foot then on the other. The antique dealer answered the phone in such a loud, firm voice that Janie could hear what she said. Aunt Cissie asked about the locket with the pearls, the one that didn't open, and Mrs. Arnot said, yes, she knew which locket Aunt Cissie meant.

"I did manage to get it open at last," Mrs. Arnot said, "but if there ever was a picture or a lock of hair inside, it's gone now. The locket was empty."

"Where did you get the locket?" Aunt Cissie asked.

"Miss Perry brought it in a few months ago. I had told her I was interested in old jewellery. The locket wasn't extremely valuable, but I was satisfied to have it."

"Thank you," Aunt Cissie said faintly. She hung up before Mrs. Arnot had a chance to say good-bye.

"Miss Perry?" Janie echoed with surprise. "Miss Perry? Where would she get Cousin Emily's locket?"

Aunt Cissie and Janie looked at each other with bewilderment.

"Maybe *she's* your cousin Emily, come back to get revenge," Janie burst out with excitement. "She's trying to frighten you into leaving the house just because she couldn't have it herself."

"But, Janie," Aunt Cissie objected, "Emily would be even older than I am, and Miss Perry is much younger. Why, she can't be forty —"

"Maybe she just stayed young looking," Janie persisted. "Maybe she dyed her hair — and you know how she always says she's watching her figure so she won't get fat. Maybe she's really *old*."

"She couldn't hide that many years," Aunt Cissie declared.

Janie frowned. Then she had another idea. "Maybe she's Cousin Emily's daughter!" As soon as she said this, Janie knew it made sense. Miss Perry would be about the right age to be a child of Cousin Emily's.

The room was very silent. Aunt Cissie was trying to think about what Janie had said. Janie was so stunned by her own idea and how right it seemed that she didn't say anything more for a moment. She stared into Aunt Cissie's faded blue eyes intently, waiting to see what Aunt Cissie would think, what she would say.

"But — but —" Aunt Cissie shook her head as though to clear her mind. Then she closed her eyes as if it were all too much for her to try to sort out and make sense of.

"Maybe Cousin Emily told her daughter about growing up here and how she felt cheated because she didn't inherit the house or any of the money. Then one day her daughter — Miss Perry — came to this town and saw you living in the house — oh, it could be that way, Aunt Cissie!"

When Aunt Cissie did not answer, Janie went on urgently. "Do you remember how Miss Perry happened to start working for Mrs. Witticomb?"

"Let me see." Aunt Cissie frowned to herself. "It was about three years ago. Mrs. Witticomb met Miss Perry working as secretary to a man who owned a seaside resort where Mrs. Witticomb went one summer. They became friends, and when Mrs. Witticomb returned from her vacation she offered Miss Perry the job. Miss Perry apparently preferred that kind of work to the work at the resort."

"Maybe it was Mrs. Witticomb's town that really interested her," Janie said. "Maybe when Mrs. Witticomb said she was from Fairfield, Miss Perry was curious to see where her mother had grown up. Maybe Mrs. Witticomb even mentioned knowing you."

"That wouldn't have meant much to Miss Perry. I mean, if she is Emily's daughter. She wouldn't have recognized the name Mariott. I wasn't married until a long time after Emily left."

"Well, maybe so," Janie admitted, "but she would know where the house was, and after she came she would know you were her mother's cousin."

"But, Janie, to do all those dreadful things —" Aunt Cissie started to say.

But Janie was rushing on. "She could have

written you the letters and made the phone calls. Don't you remember that the day of the quilt sale she wasn't with us all the time? She could have come here and pretended to search the house and left that note just to scare you more, And the day we went to Mrs. Witticomb's house Miss Perry went out to do some errands, she *said*. She could have come back here and messed up the pantry."

"How could she have got into the house?" Aunt Cissie objected. "I remember locking the back door myself that afternoon, while we were waiting for Mrs. Witticomb to come."

Janie thought a moment, trying to bring back the afternoon in every detail. "Miss Perry brought the empty tea glasses to the kitchen just before we left for the drive. She could have unlocked the door again while she was alone in the kitchen."

Aunt Cissie looked dumbly at Janie. It was so hard for her to understand all this — that anyone could want to do things like that.

"And she could have called up Mr. Follett," Janie said, "and imitated your voice. She could have come in the front door while we were sitting on the back porch watching for Mr. Follett. She could have brought in the snake, and locked us in the parlour, and turned off the electricity, and then gone back down the road where she had left her car and driven back here and pretended just to be driving by. She could have done everything, Aunt Cissie."

"But you may be mistaken about the locket, Janie. It may just be one that looks like Cousin Emily's."

"Let's go to the shop, and you can see it for yourself, Aunt Cissie. You'd recognise it, wouldn't you?"

Aunt Cissie answered slowly. "Yes, Janie, I think I would know Cousin Emily's locket if I saw it."

Mrs. Arnot seemed surprised to see Aunt Cissie and Janie coming into her shop. She was working in an account book, and she looked up when she heard the bell over the door. Janie and Aunt Cissie stood hesitantly by the door, letting their eyes grow accustomed to the dimness. Mrs. Arnot took off her glasses and came toward the front of the shop.

They were alone. There were no other customers today. The shop was very quiet. It was easy for Janie to feel the oldness of the things in the shop. The past histories and yesterdays that were gone seemed to be there in the dimness, in the shine of light across an old table, the creak of a rocker as Mrs. Arnot passed it, the tick of a clock somewhere in the silence.

"This is a surprise, Mrs. Mariott," Mrs. Arnot said. She did not even appear to notice Janie. But Janie was getting used to Mrs. Arnot's manner.

"I thought I would like to look at that locket I spoke to you about," Aunt Cissie said. "It sounds like one that once belonged to someone I knew."

"Is that so?" Mrs. Arnot sensed a sale. "Right over here," she said, going to the table at the side of the shop where Janie had looked at the old rings and lockets. She opened the box and began to look for the locket Aunt Cissie wanted to see. For a moment Janie could not see it in the box, and she had the horrid thought that it might be missing somehow. But no, there it was. Mrs. Arnot lifted it from amidst the other things and straightened the long, gold chain.

"Here it is." She held it out toward Aunt Cissie.

Aunt Cissie took the locket gently in her hands. Janie could see that her fingers trembled as they touched the smooth, pale gold of the locket. The ring of pearls shone softly in the light. Mrs. Arnot watched curiously as

Aunt Cissie held the locket closer, drawing in her breath with the surprise of recognition.

"Yes — yes, I remember this — she used to wear it often —"

Mrs. Arnot's expression was one of interest, but she did not say anything. Janie pressed close against Aunt Cissie and looked at the locket again. It was exactly the same as the one in the photograph of Cousin Emily. She wondered what Aunt Cissie would do now.

Aunt Cissie did not do anything for what seemed to Janie a long time. She stood looking at the locket, rubbing the smooth gold with one finger, her mind travelling back over the years. Then at last she said, "May I take this for a while, Mrs. Arnot? I know someone whom I think would be interested in seeing it."

"Why, yes, of course." Mrs. Arnot's manner was businesslike. She was sure a sale was in the offing. "Take it by all means and show your friend."

Aunt Cissie looked up at that and smiled regretfully at Mrs. Arnot.

"It's not exactly a friend, I'm afraid," she said softly. Her voice sounded sad to Janie. She had thought Aunt Cissie would be angry with Miss Perry — if it was Miss Perry who had been frightening her these past weeks. But Aunt Cissie did not sound angry, only sad.

Mrs. Arnot was puzzled by Aunt Cissie's reply, but again she refrained from asking any questions. For a moment her gaze rested upon Janie, as if she were seeing her for the first time. When Janie's eyes met hers, Mrs. Arnot nodded and even smiled a small smile. Janie smiled back. Somehow she did not feel so awed of Mrs. Arnot now, or blame her for wanting to buy Aunt Cissie's house.

Janie and Aunt Cissie went out again, into the silent summer morning. The sun had gone, and a hushed, waiting greyness hung overhead. The streets were almost deserted. Aunt Cissie carried the locket in her handbag and held the sturdy black straps tightly.

"What will we do now?" Janie whispered.

But Aunt Cissie didn't hear. She got into her car and drove in an easterly direction along the street. Janie knew they were not heading back to Aunt Cissie's house, but that was all she could be sure of. She did not know her way around town well enough to guess where Aunt Cissie was going. She sat quietly in the front seat beside Aunt Cissie, every now and then glancing down at her aunt's handbag on the seat between them, to be sure it was still there safe and sound with the locket inside. After a while she decided they were going to the police station. But she was wrong. Aunt Cissie drew to a stop before Mrs. Witticomb's house. Janie felt the skin prickle along her arms.

Aunt Cissie did not get out of the car at once. It was a time to measure each act and word with care, and once she had stopped the car she sat very still. Finally, when Janie felt she could not wait a minute longer, Aunt Cissie gripped the handles of her handbag and opened the door on her side and hopped out quickly.

Aunt Cissie walked slowly but without hesitation up the walk to Mrs. Witticomb's front steps.

Ghosts

Aunt Cissie rang the doorbell. Janie felt her heartbeat quicken with excitement. She peered up at Aunt Cissie, but Aunt Cissie stood looking straight ahead at the door.

It was Miss Perry herself who opened the door. From the room beyond, Janie heard Mrs. Witticomb call, "Who is it, Miss Perry?"

"It's Mrs. Mariott and Janie —" Miss Perry began to say, but by that time Aunt Cissie was walking towards the parlour doorway. Mrs. Witticomb sat on a sofa reading a newspaper. She lowered the paper when she saw Aunt Cissie and Janie.

"What brings you out so early?" Mrs. Witticomb asked with pleased surprise. She patted the sofa cushion for Janie to come and sit by her, but Janie stayed close beside Aunt Cissie.

"Whatever is the matter?" Mrs. Witticomb asked suddenly. "Why, Cissie, you're white as a sheet."

"Am I?" Aunt Cissie sat down in the first handy chair, keeping her handbag firmly on her lap.

"You look as if you'd just seen a ghost," Mrs. Witticomb said.

"I have," Aunt Cissie replied.

Mrs. Witticomb looked at her sharply and somewhat apprehensively. "Miss Perry, bring Mrs. Mariott some water, she looks faint —"

"No." Aunt Cissie turned to Miss Perry and held up her hand. "No, I don't need any water, thank you. I'm quite all right."

"You look faint," Mrs. Witticomb insisted.

But Aunt Cissie shook her head. "I've brought something to show Miss Perry," she said. "Something I thought she would be interested in seeing." She opened the clasp of her handbag, a loud click in the sudden silence of the room. Janie watched Miss Perry's face as Aunt Cissie drew the locket from the handbag and carefully folded back the white tissue paper Mrs. Arnot had wrapped around it.

Miss Perry's mouth fell open with astonishment. Her eyes widened. But it was only for an instant. Almost as quickly as the astonishment covered her face, it was gone. She made a great effort and succeeded in hiding her surprise.

"My, what a pretty locket," she said.

Mrs. Witticomb leaned forward in her chair and frowned. She could not guess what was going on, and she did not like to be in the dark about things.

"Yes, it's very pretty," Aunt Cissie said. She looked at Miss Perry, but not angrily. Her expression was one of sorrow and bewilderment. "It once belonged to my cousin Emily, and I wish you would tell me how it came into your possession — and why you have been trying to frighten me. How could you have hated me so much?"

This time Miss Perry could not cover her feelings. Her mouth opened again, and her look was startled. A flush of red swept her face from the roots of her hair. She moved forward and snatched the locket from Aunt Cissie so quickly that Aunt Cissie did not have time to draw it away. The tissue paper fluttered to the floor. The chain on the locket rattled with a soft metallic sound.

"Yes, I'm Emily's daughter! It was my mother's locket," Miss Perry blurted out. Her voice was unsteady, but there was an angry ring to it. "It was my mother's locket, one of the few things she had that she wasn't deprived of —"

"I never deprived her of anything," Aunt Cissie protested. "She could have stayed with me as long as she wanted, forever if that was what she wanted. She could have shared Dark Wood with me."

"But it wouldn't really have been hers, would it?" Miss Perry forced the words out between tightly pressed lips. "When it came down to something that really mattered there was nothing for my mother, nothing. She had to work for every cent she ever had. That house should have been half hers."

"She could have —"

But Miss Perry interrupted Aunt Cissie. "I mean half hers legally, in writing, in black and white. Then she might have stayed and shared it with you."

As suddenly as she had started talking, she stopped. She turned away from Aunt Cissie, although not before Janie saw tears glisten in her eyes. But Janie could not quite believe that anyone in her right mind could do the truly horrid things that Miss Perry had done.

"I'm sorry for you," Aunt Cissie said. "You

must have hated me very much, to want to drive me out of the only home I've ever known."

"I didn't hate you," Miss Perry stammered. She seemed distracted and hardly able to say what she thought or felt toward anyone. "When I came to work for Mrs. Witticomb, I thought I had forgotten all the things my mother had felt so bitter about before she died. But when I saw you, living so comfortably — as you had all these years — in that house my mother had loved — I wanted you to be unhappy, like she was."

"Your mother loved Dark Wood?" Aunt Cissie's tone said that she had never thought of this.

"Of course she loved it," Miss Perry answered in a strained voice. "Just as much as you did. She had grown up there, she thought of it as her home just as much as you did. She told me about sitting on the back porch steps to shell peas before dinnertime — and what she could see from the window of her bedroom, the woods across the road and the apple tree that grew by the side of the house. She told me about stringing lights on the Christmas trees, and how much she loved the piano in the parlour, and the bay window in the dining room. She liked to sit there and read, curled up on the window seat behind the curtains, all by herself. No one could see her when she sat there. It was her secret place."

There were tears in Aunt Cissie's eyes now, too. "Yes," she murmured, "I remember all those things."

Miss Perry stood with her back to the others, her head cast down, the locket clutched tightly between her fingers, the slender gold chain swinging down.

"Why did you sell the locket?" Aunt Cissie asked at last.

Miss Perry was making an effort not to cry. Janie could see her moving her fingers on her cheeks to rub away the tear streaks.

"I don't know," she said. Her voice sounded weary. "I was in the antique shop one day and saw the old rings and things that Mrs. Arnot has, and I remembered this locket of my mother's. I thought perhaps it was foolish to cling so sentimentally to old things from the past. I suppose in a way I was trying to make a break with all the unhappy memories —"

No one said anything for a long time. Then Mrs. Witticomb sat back, her dress rustling softly.

"I'll go away," Miss Perry said finally.

No one answered her. They all seemed to know this would be best. Aunt Cissie did not want to make public what had happened. After all, Miss Perry was her cousin's child. She did not want to go to the police. And she was not frightened any longer. No one was going to drive her from Dark Wood.

Aunt Cissie would not be selling her house. There would be many more summers ahead when Janie could come to visit, just as she always had. From her window she would see the woods across the road. She could sit on the back porch steps in the sunlight and wade in the river and run in the fields. There was nothing to frighten Aunt Cissie any longer. She had lived in the old country house since the day she was born, and she could live in it until the day she died. Just as she had always said she would.

Janie watched the dangling chain of the locket . . . and for a moment it seemed that someone else was with them in the room. Someone who had once been a little girl with a plain face and straight brown hair. Someone growing up in a house in the country, seeing the woods across the road and the apple tree blooming below her window . . . but drawing herself away behind the curtains, quietly and

secretly, and then by and by going away forever to hide a hurt no one could soothe. Janie
could almost see her, a girl with a dark-eyed,
solemn face. And on the front of her dress was
the gleam of a gold locket with a circle of
pearls.